The Sleep Tight Book

William L. Coleman

Photos by Dick Easterday, Aileen Bledsoe, and Fred Renich

BETHANY HOUSE PUBLISHERS
MINNEAPOLIS, MINNESOTA 55438
A Division of Bethany Fellowship, Inc.

Verses marked TLB are taken from *The Living Bible*, copyright 1971 by Tyndale House Publishers, Wheaton, Ill. Used by permission.

Published by Bethany House Publishers
A Division of Bethany Fellowship, Inc.
6820 Auto Club Road, Minneapolis, Minnesota 55438

Printed in the United States of America

Library of Congress Cataloging in Publication Data

Coleman, William L.
  The sleep tight book.

  Summary: Fifty-two short bedtime readings on night, sleep, and other comforting themes.
  1. Children—Prayer-books and devotions—
English. [1. Prayer books and devotions. 2. Sleep. 3. Night] I. Title.
BV4870.C636   1982   242'.62   82-12953
ISBN 0-87123-577-3

Acknowledgment

A special thanks to June Coleman for reading and correcting this manuscript.

About the Author

WILLIAM L. COLEMAN is becoming increasingly well known as a gifted writer and author. He has written a number of devotionals for families with young children (listed at the back of this book). He has also begun an adventure-mystery series for ages 8-15, of which three titles are available.

Coleman is a graduate of Washington Bible College in Washington, D.C., and Grace Theological Seminary in Winona Lake, Indiana. He has pastored three churches and he is a Staley Foundation lecturer. His articles have appeared in several well-known evangelical magazines. He lives in Aurora, Nebraska, with his wife and three children.

Table of Contents

Introduction

Have a Good Night

Nights are terrific
For children, beetles, owls,
Grandparents, skunks and porcupines.

The night is filled
With amazing changes
And fascinating events
We seldom get to see.

God gave us the night
Because He knew
It was good for us.

Cuddle up in a comfortable bed.
Close your eyes and listen.
The night is a fascinating time.

William L. Coleman
Aurora, Nebraska

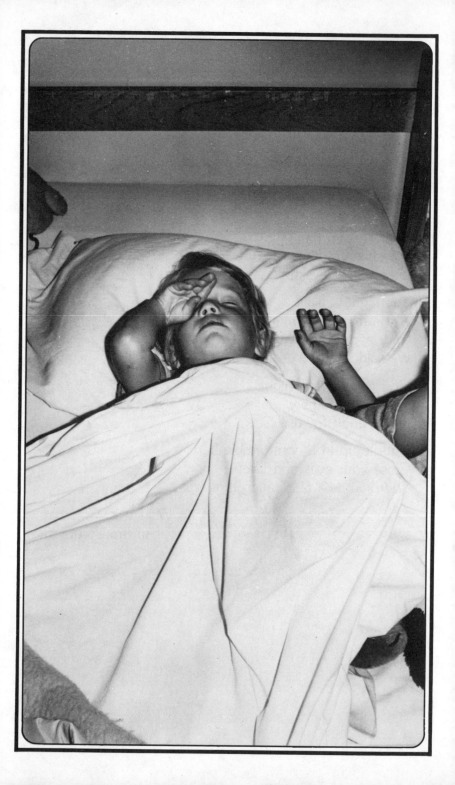

The Sandman Comes

When you wake up tomorrow,
You will probably have
Tiny pieces of "sand"
In the corners of your eyes,
Near your nose.

We used to say
The sandman comes
During the night
And puts sand in our eyes.

This "sand" really comes
From an oily liquid
That protects our eyes—
In the daytime
And while we are asleep.

This oil keeps our tears
From leaking out of our eyes.
But, if the tears begin to flow too much,
They can get through the seal.

This oil also keeps air
From getting into our eyes
While we are asleep.

The seal is very light
And will break open
The minute you wake up.

The dry oil isn't really from
The sandman.
It is the protection
God puts in your eyes.

See if you can feel
The "sand"
Tomorrow morning!

You can rub
The sand out
And enjoy
The beautiful world
God has created.

"A pleasant thing it is for the eyes to behold the sun." (Eccles. 11:7, KJV)

The Good Night

The night is a good time.
While you are asleep,
The night is not dull.

There are more animals
Moving around in the dark
Than we ever see during the day.

13

The night is a beautiful time.
Stars are twinkling,
The moon lights up
The meadows, the streets,
And our backyards.

On some nights you can see
Clouds moving across the sky
With their light, gray,
And dark shades.

The night is a good time.
The night has never hurt
Anyone.

Sometimes scary stories,
Or spooky television shows,
Can make us feel afraid
Of the night.

That is why it is good
To avoid those kinds,
Especially close to bedtime.

The night doesn't need
To be scary.
The night doesn't hurt
Anyone.

Night is a good time,
Night is a restful time.

God gave us the night
As a gift.

Have a good night.

"Day and night alike belong to you; You made the starlight and the sun." (Ps. 74:16, TLB)

A Blanket of Snow

Most of us would not want
A blanket made of cold snow.
We enjoy the white fluffy flakes,
But we wouldn't want to sleep under it!

However, snow does make a good blanket.
Many insects need the snow
To keep them warm
During the cold winter.

Some insects bury themselves
In the ground
And sleep there
All winter.

If the weather gets too cold,
Many of the insects will die.
A cold blanket of snow
Will keep the ground
From getting too cold.

Often an insect
Is still in its egg
While it is in the ground.

They need the snow
To keep the eggs
From freezing.

A snow blanket
May not be your idea
Of warmth.
But for insects,
It is just what they need.

When you cuddle up
In your warm blanket
During the winter,
Be glad you aren't
An insect—
Sleeping under the snow!

"He sends the snow in all its lovely whiteness." (Ps. 147:16, TLB)

A Good Memory

How good is your memory?
Can you remember
What you had for breakfast today?

Can you remember
What color socks you wore? (without looking)
Can you remember
What time you got up this morning?

You have a good memory.
Sometimes you forget,
But most of the time
Your memory works well.

Birds and insects
Don't seem to have
As good a memory
As you do.
But many seem to find
The same place to sleep
As they did the night before.

Some bumblebees go back
To the same flower every night
As long as the flower lasts.

Birds can "remember" where
They slept last night,
And go back to the same branch.

Butterflies can travel
Around all day,
And at night find
The same piece of bark
They found the night before.

Memories are great.
They allow us to think
About the people we love
When they are not around.

God has a great memory.
He never forgets you.
He promises to watch over you
Day and night.
Sleep tight!

"He is the God who keeps every promise." (Ps. 146:6, TLB)

God's Love

When does God love us the most?
Does God love you more
When you behave well
And do everything right?

God loves you all the time!

Does God love you less
When you have done something wrong?
When you break a cup,
Or disobey your parents,
Does God feel differently about you?

God loves you all the time!

Does God love you when
You are playing with friends,
Or watching television,
Or looking for your cat?

God loves you all the time!

Does God love you when
You are sound asleep,
Wrapped warmly in the covers
With your head resting peacefully
On your pillow?

God loves you all the time!

God's love doesn't
Come and go.
He doesn't love you
One minute
And not love you
The next minute.

God loves you all the time!

God loves you tonight
While you are sleeping.

Good night, God.

"Your love for us continues on forever." (Ps. 106:1, TLB)

Safe Inside

It feels good
To be inside
While you sleep
Through the night.

At night
A strange animal,
All black and white,
Roams around
In the woods.

It walks with a waddle.
It is called a skunk.
A skunk probably won't
Hurt people,
But it does have a strong smell!

If it meets someone
In the dark, and is frightened,
A skunk might
Lift its rear legs
And shoot an awful liquid.

If necessary,
A skunk can shoot
Five or six times!

It could spray
All the way across
Your bedroom.

The stink from a skunk
Is so powerful,
You can smell it
Half a mile away.

The smell from a skunk
Is a good reason
To be safely inside
A house,
A tent,
A trailer,
Or someplace
Where a skunk
Can't spray you.

A warm, dry bed
Is a good place to be
In the middle of the night.

"The homes are safe from every fear." (Job 21:9, TLB)

Sleeping with the Animals

Can you imagine a lion
So calm and friendly
That you could take
A real one
To bed with you
And not be afraid?

What if your teddy bear
Was a big, live one,
And you could wrap
Your arm around its neck
And go to sleep
And not be afraid?

Today it is too dangerous
To go to sleep with
Wild animals.
But someday, children like you
Will be able to sleep next to
A huge tiger
And not be afraid!

Someday, God will change
The world—
And all of its creatures.

God will bring peace
Between people
And among animals.

Then the fox
Will crawl into a bed,
Or a child will crawl
Into the bed
Of a leopard.

Some children
Will trade
Their stuffed animals
For real ones!

"At that time I will make a treaty between you and the wild animals, birds, and snakes, not to fear each other any more; and I will destroy all weapons, and all wars will end. Then you will lie down in peace and safety, unafraid." (Hosea 2:18, TLB)

A Long-Necked Ostrich

When bedtime comes,
The ostrich
Has a gigantic problem.
Where will the tall ostrich
Put its head?

Sometimes they lie down.
But they get up often
During the night.
On some nights
An ostrich
Gets up 16 times.

Many times
The ostrich
Will go to sleep standing.
However, it gets so tired
That it puts its head
On a fence, or
Lays it flat on the ground.

When an ostrich is sound asleep,
You can walk up to it
And yell.
But the ostrich will
Keep on sleeping.

When a group of ostriches
Are sleeping together,
One ostrich stays awake.
It is ready to warn the others
If trouble comes.

We don't all go to sleep
At the same time, either.
Parents usually stay up
After the children are asleep.

There are policemen and firemen
Who stay awake all night.
They are ready to help
If we need them.

You can go to sleep tonight.
Others are awake
To keep watch in the night.

The night is a time
To sleep
Peacefully.

"He protects you day and night."

(Ps. 121:6, TLB)

Tossing and Turning

It can be miserable
When you can't sleep.
You stare at the dark ceiling;
You roll to one side
And then the other.

Some nights
You might count sheep,
Or tell stories to yourself.
Maybe you will pretend
You are a sea captain,
Or a mountain climber,
Or even an astronaut.

All of us have trouble
Going to sleep, sometimes.
That's all right.

Maybe you ate too much,
Or are too excited
About tomorrow,
Or you might be *too* tired.

Maybe you have a fear.
Maybe you have a question.
Maybe you feel confused.
Maybe you have something
You need to tell someone.

Tonight you might sleep better
If you could talk to someone
Before you turn out the lights.

You might like to tell God
What is on your mind.
You might like to tell a parent
What you are thinking.

Sometimes we sleep so much better
After we talk to someone.

"I love the Lord because he hears my prayers and answers them."
(Ps. 116:1, TLB)

Someone to Hug

Have you ever gone to sleep
In the arms of your mother or father?
It is such a good feeling
To go to sleep touching someone
You love.

Parents enjoy it, too.
They like the feeling
Of their child sound asleep
In their arms.

Animals often like this, too.
Otters can sleep on their backs
Floating in a river.
Sometimes a mother otter
Will float in the water, asleep,
With a baby otter
Resting its head
On the mother otter's side.

They float and sleep together,
Touching each other peacefully.
The mother otter will wake up,
Gently pet the baby otter,
And go back to sleep.

Sometimes we get busy
And forget to hug each other.
But it feels terrific
When a child climbs up
Into his parent's lap
And goes to sleep
In his arms.

Before you go to sleep tonight,
You might want to sit on
Someone's lap,
Or hug someone,
Or give him
A kiss.

Thank God
That you
Have someone
To hug.

"So he returned home to his father. And while he was still a long distance away, his father saw him coming, and was filled with loving pity and ran and embraced him and kissed him."

(Luke 15:20, TLB)

32

A Dolphin's Bed

Does anyone in your family
Own a water bed?
They aren't a new idea.
Dolphins have always slept
On water beds!

When a dolphin goes to sleep,
It rests just under the surface
Of the water.
Dolphins have to breathe,
So every minute or more
They float up
And take a breath.

They go to sleep,
But only for a minute or two
At a time.

This might not be
The way you want
To sleep,
But it works great
For a dolphin.

Since it lives in the water,
A dolphin does not seem to need
As much sleep
As human beings.

But dolphins do not spend their day
Climbing stairs, or wrestling.
All day long
The water holds their bodies up.

If a dolphin decides
To take a trip,
He does not have to take
A sleeping bag along—
He is already
In his bed.

Dolphins do not have to
Carry their covers, either.
The water cover is a part
Of their bed.

Do you have a soft,
Comfortable, warm bed
To sleep in tonight?

You can lie there quietly
And think about the amazing world
God has created.

The dolphins are in bed now, too.
Beds are nice places to be.

"Lie quietly upon your bed in silent meditation." (Ps. 4:4, TLB)

Enjoying Gifts

Isn't it fun to get a gift?
Something you didn't have to buy,
But that someone gave you
Just because he likes you.

Gifts are especially fun
If they are wrapped.
You probably like to tear open the paper
And open the box.

However, a gift doesn't *have*
To be wrapped
To be fun.
As long as you like the gift,
It brings a big smile
To your face.

Then you remember
Who gave you the gift,
And you thank them—
Because they are really kind,
And thoughtful,
And loving.

Gifts are great to get,
And they are nice to give.

Tonight you can have
A special, bedtime gift.
It won't be wrapped.
You can't wind it up,
And it won't fit
On your dresser.

While you go to sleep,
God will give you a gift—
Peace.

You don't have to worry
About tonight,
Or tomorrow,
Or next week.

Because God
Gives you peace—
For tonight.

Pull up your covers,
Close your eyes,
And receive God's gift.

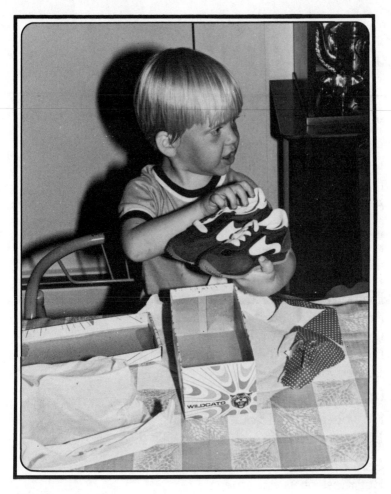

Sleep in peace.
Good night.

"I am leaving you with a gift—peace of mind and heart! And the peace I give isn't fragile like the peace the world gives. So don't be troubled or afraid." (John 14:27, TLB)

A Pillow for Your Head

How would you describe your pillow?
Is it long or short?
Does it have a white pillowcase,
A yellow, or blue one?

Is your pillow soft and fluffy,
Or is it firm and solid?

How do you sleep with your pillow?
Do you wrap your arms around it
And hug it?
Do you roll your pillow into a ball?
Do you sleep with your head
Under your pillow?

When you wake up in the morning,
Do you ever find your pillow
Lying on the floor?

Some people do not use a pillow,
But most of us like one.
It makes our head and neck
Feel more comfortable.

It might sound silly,
But a pillow is one
Of the good things
About going to bed.
Pillows make us feel better
And help us go to sleep.

When Jesus was a child,
He probably enjoyed a good pillow
Just like you do.

Later, as an adult,
He still used one.

Maybe you had better
Get your pillow ready.
It's time to go to sleep.
Smooth it out,
Move it around,
Or fluff it into a ball.

Enjoy a quiet night
Of sleep
With your pillow.

"Jesus was asleep at the back of the boat with his head on a cushion." (Mark 4:38, TLB)

You Can Just Relax

Your body begins to get
Tired at night.
Your arms and legs and hands
Start to relax.

The night is quiet
And restful.
Soon you may be
Sound asleep.

When you go to sleep
Your hands usually
Open up,
Because there is no need
To hold onto anything.

Monkeys sleep differently
Than we do.
Their small hands
Close tightly
When they go to sleep.

A monkey might go to sleep
Sitting straight up,
Holding firmly onto a branch.
It can go to sleep
Holding on with closed fists
And sleep peacefully.

But people do not
Have to hold onto something
While they sleep.
You don't have to
Grab your bed,
Or hold onto
Your dresser
To go to sleep.

You might *want* to
Hold something,
Like a stuffed animal,
Or a doll.
But you don't *have* to
Have something.
You can just relax
And go to sleep.

You can let go,
Because God is holding
Onto you.
It's as if God
Were holding your hand—
Right now.

Tell God good night.

"But even so, you love me! You are holding my right hand!"

(Ps. 73:23, TLB)

Too Much Sleep

Some people,
If they could,
Might sleep all night
And all day as well.

Some people love to get up
And do interesting things.
Others love to sleep
And don't like to get up.

The sloth is one
Of those creatures
Who loves to sleep
All it can.

It also likes to eat,
But it enjoys sleeping
More than food.

However, the sloth does
Seem to live
To an old age
Because it isn't
In a hurry
To do anything.

Some sloths sleep
So soundly
That you could place
A paper plate
On its head,
And the next morning
It would probably
Still be there.

Sometimes we like to sleep
As much as a sloth does.
If we had our way,
We might sleep until noon.

But if we sleep
Too much,
We will miss
Too much
Of the wonderful world
That God has made.

Sleep well tonight.
But when it's morning,
Wake up and enjoy
God's fantastic world.

"A lazy fellow has trouble all through life; the good man's path is easy." (Prov. 15:19, TLB)

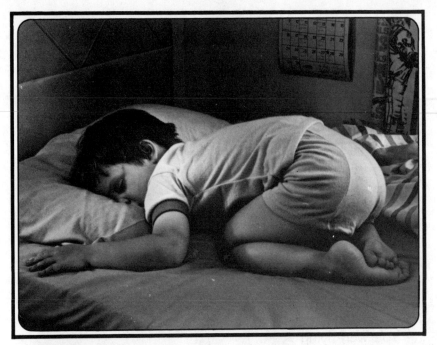

Sleeping on Your Head

How do you sleep?
Do you lie on your side
Or on your stomach?
Or do you wiggle around
Like a worm?

Some people roll up
Almost into a ball.
Others hang off the bed.
And some
Put their heads under the pillow
And raise their bodies up
As if they were standing
On their heads!

Horses are something like people
In the way they sleep.
They might wake up
In a funny position.

Often a horse will sleep
Standing up,
With its head hanging down,
Or resting on the
Top of a gate.

At other times a horse
Will lie on its side,
Or rest comfortably
On its stomach.

Have you ever thought
About the funny ways
You were lying
When you woke up?

Tell God good night now,
And in the morning
Notice how you are lying
When you wake up.

God sees you
In whatever position
You are sleeping.

He smiles at you.
Because He loves you.

"O God, in mercy bless us; let your face beam with joy as you look down at us." (Ps. 67:1, TLB)

A Cricket Concert

When you pull up your covers
For a long night's sleep,
The crickets play a concert
To keep you company.

Some people enjoy
Cricket music so much,
They capture the small insects,
And keep them in a cage.
At night they can listen
To the tiny orchestra.

There are some cricket listeners
Who claim you can tell the temperature
By counting a cricket's chirps.

Do you want to try it?
Count the number of chirps
From a snow cricket
For fifteen seconds.
Then add 40 to the
Number you get.

For instance,
If you count 30 chirps
In 15 seconds,
And add 40,
The temperature
Is 70 degrees.

Snow crickets are found
In many areas.
If the weather is too cool

Or too hot,
They do not chirp.

The warmer the evening,
The more chirps
You will hear.

There are many animals
And small creatures
Singing and playing
While you sleep
Tonight.

Before you go to sleep,
You might enjoy
Singing a song, too.

**"But the people of God will sing a
song of solemn joy, like songs in
the night."** (Isa. 30:29, TLB)

The Fields at Night

Our bodies change at night.
Our bones take a rest.
Even our muscles relax,
So they can be stronger
For the next day.

While we are sleeping,
The plants in the fields
Are changing, too.

Plants don't really sleep
The way we do,
But they do change
At night.

When the sun goes down,
The sugar in a ripe ear of corn
Starts to flow down
The stalk.
The sugar seems to rest
At the roots
When night comes.

As the sun comes up
In the morning,
The sugar in the corn
Travels up into the plant again.

For this reason,
Some people think
Corn tastes best
When picked about one hour
After the sun comes up.

Other plants also change
When nighttime comes.
Some fold up their leaves;
Flowers close their petals
As if they were pulling up
Their covers
For the night.

The same God who loves
The plants around your house
And in the fields
Is the God who loves you
Tonight.

The plants are changing,
The petals are closed.
Close your eyes
And let your body rest.

"And if God cares so wonderfully for flowers that are here today and gone tomorrow, won't he more surely care for you, O men of little faith?" (Matt. 6:30, TLB)

Summer Visitors

When you are asleep
During the summer,
Many visitors stop by
Your window.

They might jump or fly past,
Or they may stop for a while
On your window or screen.

These tiny creatures
Are called insects.

God must have a great imagination
To have created so many kinds of insects
In such a large number of sizes and shapes.

Insects are very different from us.
Their spines run up the front
Of their bodies
Instead of the backs.
They don't have red blood,
But white, or green!

Their mouths are different from ours.
You might see two sets of jaws,
And they could be moving
Across instead of up and down.

Insects are so "mixed up"
They often hear with their knees,
Taste with their feet,
And sing with their wings.

God is an amazing creator.
Plants, animals, and bugs
Are full of surprises.

You could study them
For years and still
Find them fascinating.

After making all these creatures,
God still had so much imagination
That He made
All kinds of people.

You are so special,
There is no one
Exactly like you.

Tell your parents good night.
Tell the insects good night.
Tell God good night.

"O Lord, what a variety you have made! And in wisdom you have made them all! The earth is full of your riches." (Ps. 104:24, TLB)

Breakfast Is Coming

When you wake up tomorrow,
You will probably start the day
With a good breakfast.

Eating breakfast is a healthy habit;
It makes your day go better.

What is your favorite breakfast food?
Do you like eggs, toast, or bacon?
Maybe you enjoy cereal.
Do you like it best hot or cold?

We don't have to get up early
And go out looking for our food.
But many animals spend most of the night
Searching for something to eat.

The prickly porcupine is one animal
That looks for food during the night.
It likes to eat leaves
Or munch on tree bark.

Some animals try to attack porcupines,
But they could end up with
Some long, pointed quills
Stuck in the paw, side or jaw.

Porcupines do not throw quills,
But they strike with the tail—
Sticking a handful of painful quills
Into the attacker.

For many animals,
The search for food

54

Is a very hard task,
And sometimes dangerous.

God has given us
Parents or other adults
To care for us
And to provide our food.

We should be thankful
To wake up to
A good breakfast
On the table.

"He gives food to every living thing, for his lovingkindness continues forever." (Ps. 136:25, TLB)

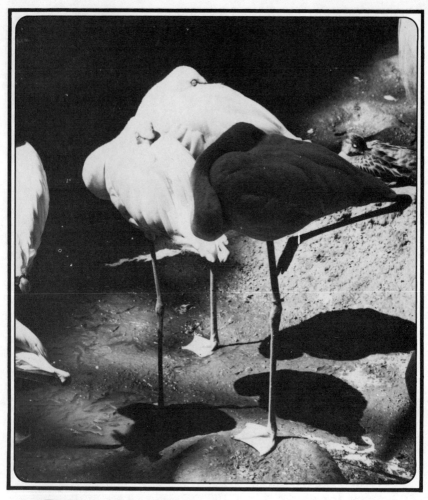

Sleeping on One Leg

Certain birds probably enjoy
Sleeping this way.
But you might not like
Sleeping all night
Standing on one foot!

The plump goose
Often lifts one leg
And goes to sleep
Standing on the other leg.

Canaries can sleep
Any number of ways.
They have been seen
Roosting like a chicken,
Or lying on their sides
On a cage floor.

However, you might also see
A canary standing
On one leg—
Sound asleep.

Sleeping on one leg
Might be easy for birds,
But most of us enjoy
Lying down,
Cuddled under our blankets,
Fast asleep.

Doesn't your bed feel good?

"I myself will be the Shepherd of my sheep, and cause them to lie down in peace, the Lord God says." (Ezek. 34:15, TLB)

Almost Dawn

While you are still sleeping
The sun will begin to rise,
The darkness will clear away,
And nature will start to change.

Dawn is coming.
Before long,
You will wake up.

On most mornings,
The night creatures
Will be settled in their beds
Before you wake up.

The night owl will go
Back into its tree-hole,
And the worms will crawl
Back into the ground.

Dawn is coming.

Dandelions will start opening,
And beetles will wiggle
Beneath a stone,
Or snuggle into a rotted log.

Early morning is a busy time,
With creatures scurrying
In many directions
Looking for their daytime beds.

If you look at the rooftops,
You might see a night hawk
Which has perched there
To rest for the day.

If you turn over a leaf,
You might find a firefly

Quietly waiting
For the darkness to return.

While much of nature
Is going to bed,
You will be waking up
To a terrific morning
And a great day.

**"Let me see your kindness to me
in the morning, for I am trusting
you. Show me where to walk,
for my prayer is sincere."**

(Ps. 143:8, TLB)

Do You Cry?

Some days, have you felt
You just had to cry?
Maybe you hurt yourself
And the pain was awful.

Maybe someone yelled at you,
And your feelings were hurt.
Maybe you did something wrong,
And your parents had to
Punish you.

When crying is necessary,
It's all right to cry.
Parents and other adults
All cry sometimes.

But crying is hard.
It makes us feel bad.
Have you ever cried
In your bed,
Or cried
Yourself to sleep?

Sometimes, after you cry,
It feels so good
Just to go to sleep.

"Tears came to Jesus' eyes."

(John 11:35, TLB)

Playing with Shadows

Do you ever like to play
With shadows in your room?
It's easy if a light
Is coming through your window.

Often the moon
Will make it easy
To make shadows.

If you use your hands,
You can make a rabbit
With long, straight ears.

You can make the shadow
Of an Indian teepee,
Or a lizard's mouth
On your wall.

Children are very creative.
They can design many things
Even with the shadows
On their walls.

There is another shadow
In your room,
But no one can see it.
It is the shadow of God.
He stays very near to us.

"We live within the shadow of the Almighty, sheltered by the God who is above all gods." (Ps. 91:1, TLB)

Your Nose at Night

If you lie still,
You can hear yourself
Breathe at night.

It isn't very loud,
But you can hear
The air traveling
In and out
Of your nose.

Imagine if you had
A nose like
The giant anteater.

They have long,
Thin noses.
They use their noses
To smell termites.

When they find
These little insects,
They stick their
Long noses
Into the termites'
Tiny homes.

We don't need
Such long noses,
But our short ones
Make good passages
For air to pass through.

God put breath
Into us,

And our noses
Help keep it going.

Tonight while you
Lie in bed
Waiting to go to sleep,
Remember the
Wonderful Creator
Who put breath
Into you.

Have a
Good night's
Sleep.

**"He himself gives life and breath
to everything, and satisfies every
need there is."** (Acts 17:25, TLB)

Close Your Eyes

If would be awful
If you had to keep
Your eyes open all night.

You couldn't rest or sleep;
You would be
Just staring into the dark.

When we sleep,
We can simply
Close our eyes
And relax.

Sometimes birds sleep
Without closing
Their eyes.

Birds have three eyelids.
They are called
Uppers, lowers and blinkers.

The blinker eyelid
Is the tricky one.
A bird can close
Its blinker lid
And look like
It is asleep.

However, the bird
Can see through
Its blinker lid.

A cat might try
To sneak up on it,
But the bird can
Actually see the cat.

When a bird's eyes
Are closed,
They might really
Be open.

We people can't do that.
We can close our eyes,
And seeing nothing,
Peacefully go to sleep.

But not everyone
Closes his eyes.
God's eyes are always open.
He sees us
And watches over us

Even when we
Are asleep.

You can close
Your eyes now
And go to sleep.

**"He closely watches everything
that happens here on earth."**
(Ps. 11:4, TLB)

A Fish's Bed

How would you
Describe your bed?
Is it long or short?
Is your mattress
Hard or soft?

What color
Are your blankets?
Do you have
More than one
Blanket on your bed?

You can be glad
You don't sleep
In the bed
Of a carp fish.

A carp sleeps
During the winter.
Before he goes to sleep,
A carp wiggles itself
Into the mud
At the bottom
Of a lake.

Almost completely buried,
The carp's heart
Slows down,
And its body temperature
Drops very low.

A carp's sleep
Is called hibernation.
It might last
For a month.

The carp's comfortable
Mud bed
Might be one reason
Why some carp live
To be one hundred years old.

For us, it is more fun
To sleep in a dry,
Warm, snuggly bed.

A bed is a good
Quiet place
To think about
All the good things
We have.

A bed is a good,
Quiet place
To think about
God
And all He has
Taught us.

"In dreams, in visions of the night when deep sleep falls on men as they lie on their beds. He opens their ears in times like that, and gives them wisdom and instruction." (Job 33:15, 16, TLB)

Sleeping Together

Do you have a brother or a sister?
Do you ever sleep together?
Maybe you sleep together regularly.

Brothers and sisters can be a nuisance.
Sometimes they take things without asking.
Sometimes they talk too much.
And once in a while
They are too loud.

Brothers and sisters can be fun
To sleep with.
They like to tell stories,

Or answer hard questions,
Or make good plans for tomorrow.

Raccoons like to sleep
With their families.
They spend months
Sleeping together
High in a hollow tree.

Bear cubs enjoy sleeping together
With their mother.
However, when they get older,
They move away
And sleep all alone.

Brothers and sisters are neat people.
They can be very helpful.
And when they want to be,
They can be fun to be with.

All of us can have a special brother
If we want Him.
Jesus told us that we are
His brother or His sister
If we obey God.

It's terrific to have
A special brother.
Jesus Christ is your brother
If you believe in Him.

Tell your special brother
Good night.

"Then he added, 'Anyone who obeys my Father in heaven is my brother, sister and mother.' "
(Matt. 12:50, TLB)

Big Ears

When our room is dark
And it is hard to see,
Our ears help tell us
What is going on.

We can hear the wind blowing
In the leaves outside,
Or hear the raindrops
Falling on the window.

Some night animals
Have extra large ears
So they can pick up more sounds
During the night.

Our outer ear is called
The *pinna*.
It is the Greek word
For seashell.

Cup your hand
Behind your outer ear
To make it larger.
Often you can hear better
If the *pinna* is bigger.

Some animals have fur
Inside their ears.
Animals without fur
Inside their ears
Can usually hear better.

At night we often
Speak softly,
Or we even whisper.

It is easier to hear
Because it is quieter
At night.

It is also restful
To talk softly
As we calm down
To go to sleep.

If you want to,
You can whisper
Good night to God.

God doesn't have to
Cup His ears to hear.
God can hear us
Very well
In the night.

Before you go to sleep,
Whisper good night to God.
He won't have any trouble
Hearing you.

"Because he bends down and listens, I will pray as long as I breathe!" (Ps. 116:2, TLB)

Talk Softly

Sh-h-h!
It is time to be still.
Everything in your room
Is getting quiet.

It is time to talk softly
And let everything
Be peaceful.

Sh-h-h!
You have done enough
For this long day.

Your bed feels good,
And your stuffed animal
Or doll or cowboy
Is by your side.

Other things will have to wait
Until tomorrow.

In a few minutes
Your eyelids will start
To feel heavy.
Your arms will get tired,
And your pillow
Will feel good
Under your head.

It is better
To talk softly now,
Because soon sleep
Will start to take over.

Sleep feels good
To a tired body
And a tired mind.

Sh-h-h!
Let's be quiet
And still.
Sleep is coming.

Sleep tight.
Good night.

"I am quiet now before the Lord."
(Ps. 131:2, TLB)

A Hard Day

How did your day go?
Was it fun,
With lots of exciting things to do?

Or was it a day
Filled with hard work,
And you felt better
When the day was over?

Maybe it was
The kind of day
When you were scolded
By your parents.

Some days are difficult,
And it seems like
Everything goes wrong.

Good parents will
Help their children
By correcting them.

They tell us
When we have done
Something wrong
So we will learn
To do better
The next time.

Some hard days
When we get
Scolded or punished
Turn out to be
The best days.

Have a good night's sleep.
You learned some things today.

"Only a fool despises his father's advice; a wise son considers each suggestion." (Prov. 15:5, TLB)

Counting Sheep

When you can't go
Right to sleep,
Do you ever try
Counting things
To make yourself
Sleepy?

Some people count balloons
Floating into the sky.
Others count ships
Sailing across the ocean.

Many people count sheep.
They picture white
And black sheep
Jumping over a short fence.

Sometimes they count
Over a hundred sheep
Before they fall asleep.

In some ways
We are just like
Those sheep.

Jesus said that
We are His sheep
And He is our
Shepherd.

A shepherd
Watches over
His sheep.

Tonight we
Go to sleep
Like sheep
Who belong
To Jesus,
Our Shepherd.

"I am the Good Shepherd and know my own sheep, and they know me." (John 10:14, TLB)

How Much Sleep?

How many hours
Do you sleep
Each night?

Some children sleep
For eight hours
Or ten hours
Or more
Every night.

By the time
You are fifteen years old
You will have slept
For five or six years!

By the time
You are thirty years old
You will have slept
For ten or twelve years.

Sleeping takes
A lot of time,
But if we don't
Get enough sleep,
We might get
Grouchy,
Sick,
Or have headaches.

Sleep and rest
Are our friends.
They help us to
Get enough strength

To have a good
Tomorrow.

When God
Created the world,
He worked
For six days.

On the seventh day,
God rested, too.

Rest is a great idea.

"God rested on the seventh day of creation." (Heb. 4:4, TLB)

Surprised at Night

There are at least
365 nights every year.
They are fascinating
With their lights, sounds,
Coolness and living,
Moving creatures.

One night was like
No other one.
A group of men
Were working outside
As they usually did.

Everything seemed normal.
They were watching their sheep
To keep them safe
From other animals.

Suddenly, a bright light
Came from nowhere,
And the voice of an angel
Spoke to them.

The angel said
The Savior,
The Messiah,
The Lord,
Would be born
In Bethlehem.

The shepherds were scared
At first.
Then they heard a choir
Begin to sing.

When the choir
Finished singing,
The shepherds
Headed straight
For Bethlehem
To see
The Savior,
The Messiah,
The Lord.

It became
The most special
Night
In all their lives.

Night can be
A special time.

**"That night some shepherds were
in the fields outside the village,
guarding their flocks of sheep."**
(Luke 2:8, TLB)

You Are Not Alone

When you are sleeping
Quietly in your room,
You are really not alone.

Nature all around us
Is filled with life.
Some of nature is awake,
While some is sound asleep.

Is there a bridge
Near your home?
There might be some starlings
Asleep under there.

Is there a pond
Near your home?
There might be some ducks
Sleeping there,
Floating on the water.

Is there a bush
Near your home?
There might be some birds
Sleeping there,
Waiting for the sun to rise.

Not every creature is asleep.
Frogs might be croaking
Near the water,
And raccoons might be traveling
Through your backyard.

Nights are often quiet,
But we are not alone.

There are many creatures
Moving around, or sleeping
While we are sleeping.

We are never
Completely alone.
God keeps us company;
He stays around.

"I will never, never fail you nor forsake you." (Heb. 13:5, TLB)

Feeding the Birds

Did you get enough food today?
Do you feel full and comfortable?
Most of us get plenty to eat.
Sometimes we get too much.

The creatures around us need plenty
Of food almost every day.
Just before it became dark tonight,
The birds were hopping around
Looking for food.

They need food to help them live
Through the cold night.

Food helps give warmth
To their small bodies.

Feathers and food
Help birds on a
Very cold night.

Birds enjoy eating seeds,
But they are happy
To get bread crumbs
From a generous person.

Most of us will not have
To go out searching for food
Before we can go to bed.

We sleep with a full stomach
And a warm bed.

Before you go to sleep,
You might want to thank God
For having plenty of food.

"Give us our food again today, as usual."

(Matt. 6:11, TLB)

The Coconut Crab

What do you think of
When you hear the name
Coconut crab?

Do you picture a crab
That is round and fuzzy
And brown like a coconut?
Or do you picture a coconut
That is flat like a crab?

A coconut crab is a real crab.
But it doesn't live in the water.
Coconut crabs don't like to go
Near the water.

They live in holes
And don't like
To go out
During the day.

While you are asleep,
The coconut crab
Will climb a tree
Looking for coconuts.

It has a good name,
Because it describes exactly
What it does.
A coconut crab
Lives off coconuts.

God has many good names.
One of them
Is the name Father.

When we say

God is our Father,
We think of things like
Loving,
Helping,
Kindness,
Protecting,
Thoughtful,
Sharing,
And
Much more.

The name Father
Makes us think
So many good things
About God.

This is a good name.
Good night, Father.

**"Father, may your name be
honored."** (Luke 11:2, TLB)

Seeing in the Dark

When the lights are out
In your bedroom
Can you still see some things
Around the room?

Suppose it is very dark.
If there is no night light
Or hall light coming in
Under the door,
Can you still see some things
Around your room?

Most of us can see a few things.
Maybe we can see the end of a chair,
Part of a mirror, or the top of a dresser.

Children usually adjust to the dark
Faster than adults do.
The Vitamin A in our bodies
Helps us to see better
When we move from the light
Into a dark room.

If you lie still
For just a minute,
You might be surprised
How quickly you begin
To see in the dark.

Sometimes a cat
Will stand still
Just after it is
Put out at night.

The cat is getting used to
The new darkness.

Dogs move freely
In the dark.
Their sharp ears and
Good noses help them
Get around faster
In the dark.

All of us have
To adjust
To the darkness.
Everyone, that is, except God.

When the lights go out,
God doesn't even blink.
He can stay in the darkness
And see everything
In the room.

You can thank God
For staying close to you
When the lights go out.

"Every morning tell him, 'Thank you for your kindness,' and every evening rejoice in all his faithfulness." (Ps. 92:2, TLB)

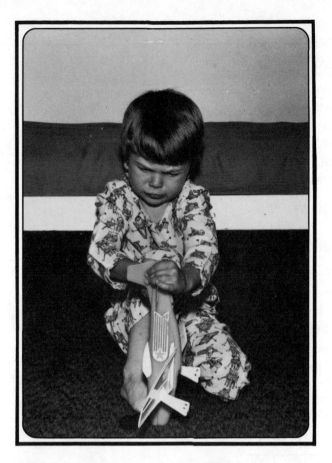

Getting Fussy

Have you ever noticed
That sometimes late at night,
Around bedtime,
It is easy to become fussy?

You might not think
You are tired,
But you may begin
To do things
Differently.

If a toy doesn't work right,
You might get mad at it.
If a brother or sister
Doesn't want to play with you,
You might get mad at them, too.

That is what is called
"Getting fussy."

When your parents tell you
To pick up your toys,
Or to turn off the television,
Do you get upset?

It happens to all of us
Sometime or other.
We get fussy.

Elijah was a prophet
Who was a good man.
But one day
After working hard,
He became fussy.

He had had enough.
Elijah didn't want
To do anything
Anymore.

Then he lay down
Under a bush
And went to sleep.

When Elijah woke up
And ate some breakfast,
He wasn't fussy
Any longer!

That might be one reason
Why God gave us sleep.

He knew it would help
When we started to get
Fussy.

Close your eyes.
When you wake up,
You will feel
Much better.

Good night!

"Then he lay down and slept beneath the broom bush."

(1 Kings 19:5, TLB)

Being Tucked In

Brian started down the hall
Toward the bedroom.
Suddenly, he stopped
And turned around.

"Be sure to come
And tuck me in!"
Brian reminded his parents.

Why do children enjoy
Being tucked in?

Many children like to have
Their mother or father
Pull their covers up
Under their chin,
Give them a goodnight kiss,
Turn off the lights,
And close the door.

It seems to be something special.
A child could pull up
His own covers
And turn out
His own light.

Many times they do it
All by themselves.

But having someone
Tuck you in
At bedtime
Is really special.

Being tucked in
Is saying,
I love you.

The person who comes
To your room
Is doing something
Nice.
They are doing something
Extra.
They are doing something
Thoughtful.

Being tucked in
Is saying,
I love you.

When your father
Or mother
Tucks you in tonight,

Tell them
You love them, too.

Being tucked in
Gives us a
Warm feeling.

"His father loves him very much."
(Gen. 44:20, TLB)

Calming Down

Do you ever get angry?
Probably everyone gets angry,
Sometimes.

Maybe a brother or sister
Took a toy of yours,
Or broke your crayons.

That made you upset.
Maybe you yelled at him
Maybe you hit him,
Maybe you took something
Of his in return.

Adults do that sometimes.
They don't break toys,
But they can get angry.

Sometimes we get mad
And stay mad for
A long time.

Did you ever stay awake
Because you were angry?
Did you ever lie in your bed
Thinking about someone
Who made you angry?

When we do that,
The anger stops us
From getting
A good night's sleep.

Bedtime is a good time
To stop being angry.

It is a good time
To forgive everyone
And forget about
What they did.

Tomorrow will be a new day.
We can start all over again,
And be friends,
And get along
Very well.

Tell your parents, "Good night."
Tell God, "Thank you."
Tell your anger, "Good-bye."

"Don't let the sun go down with you still angry—get over it quickly." (Eph. 4:26, TLB)

Are You Like a Kinkajou?

Some people are just like a Kinkajou (kin-ka-ju).
You have probably never seen one
Because they live in Central America,
South America, and Mexico.

Another reason we do not see them
Is because they roam around in the dark.

The dark sounds safe to them,
And a good time
To eat fruit.

Not many of their enemies
Are out hunting
During the night.

In the dark, a kinkajou
Loves to climb trees
And play around.

This could be a good life,
Except for one thing.
The kinkajou
Is too noisy.

They have a terrible scream
That can be heard far away.

The kinkajou would be much safer
If it would calm down
And not be so noisy.

Are you like a kinkajou?
Do you like to make noise at night,

Or do you become quiet
And rest peacefully?

It's nice to calm down,
Pull up the covers,
And enjoy the quiet night.

Just lie still,
While God
Watches over you.

"Be still and know that I am God." (Ps. 46:10, KJV)

The Long Nights

For most of us,
Each night is about
The right length.

The night is long enough
To get plenty of sleep,
And be ready to go
In the morning.

But there is a place
Where the night goes on,
And on, and on.

In the town of Deadhorse, Alaska,
The night comes, and the sun
Goes away for two months!

For sixty long days and nights
The sun refuses to shine.

It is hard to live where it is dark
Both day and night.
Many people start to argue,
And some feel discouraged.

In the summer, they have
The opposite problem.
They have sunlight
Twenty-four hours a day.

It never gets dark,
And some people can sleep
For only four or five hours.

We might like to live
Like that for a while.
However, most of us

Would rather have
Light and darkness
Every day.

The night is a good time
To get some sleep.
The light is a good time
To get up and go.

Maybe that is why
God made both of them.

"Then God said, 'Let there be light.' And light appeared. And God was pleased with it, and divided the light from the darkness." (Gen. 1:3, 4, TLB)

Hide and Seek

Where is your favorite place
To play hide and seek?
Is there a tree near your home
That is the right size
To hide behind?

Are there any bushes tall enough
To get behind and crouch down
So you can't be seen?

Some children lie down flat
On the grass.
If they don't move,
The darkness will hide them.

What do you use for a base?
Is there a lamp post
Where someone stands and counts,
Before he starts looking?

Maybe your base is a tree,
Or the side of a car,
Or the steps to your house.

Hide and seek can be played
In the daytime,
But it is much more fun
At night.

The darkness makes hiding easy.
There are shadows and dark corners
Where no one can see you.

Hide and seek would be too easy
For one person I know.
God wouldn't have any trouble

Seeing us
No matter how well we hid!

God can see through the darkness
Just as if it were noontime.

It feels good to know that.
God can always keep His eye on you.
Day or night, He is always watching you.

Thanks, God,
For watching us,
Especially in the dark.

"Darkness and light are both alike to you." (Ps. 139:12, TLB)

Good Morning

How would you describe yourself
In the morning?
Do you jump out of bed,
Happy and bright?

Are you eager to get going?
Do you come to the table
With a friendly "Hello,"
And eat a good breakfast?

Maybe you are another kind
Of person.
Do you drag out of bed?
Are you grumpy?
Do you sit at the table
Like a sad puppy?

Are you like the European Mole?
He sleeps deeply in his den.
He loves to stay asleep
In the ground.

If you find the home
Of the European Mole,
You can dig him up,
Break his home apart,
And hold him in your hands.

This mole loves sleep so much,
He will probably keep on sleeping
In your hand.

Are you like that mole?
Do you hate to get up
In the morning?

Maybe you could make tomorrow
Different.
Maybe you could hop up
Out of bed
And be happy
For such a great day.

Tomorrow will be another day
Which God has made.
Enjoy it with a song
In your heart.

"We will meet the dawn with song. I will praise you everywhere around the world." (Ps. 108:2, 3, TLB)

Feathery Coats

Can you imagine your body
Completely covered with feathers?
It might sound funny,
And maybe even itchy,
But feathers are really warm
On a cold night.

Birds stay warm
Under their feathery coats.

Feathers are designed
In a special way
To keep cold out.

The small hairs or barbs
On a feather
Hook together.
When the wind blows hard,
The feathers hold tightly.

A cold wind cannot move
Through the small barbs.

Even if a cold rain
Pours down on a bird's back,
It doesn't really bother him,
Because a bird's body produces oil,
And it spreads
All through its feathers.

When the rain falls on his back,
The water rolls off.
On a cold, wet night
A bird can stay warm
And dry.

Trusting in God
Is much like
Being under a feathery wing
On a chilly, damp night.

God is protecting,
Loving, and caring for us.
We can rest
Under His wings.

"Oh, to be safe beneath the shelter of your wings!" (Ps. 61:4, TLB)

Putting Thoughts to Bed

There are so many things
To think about.
What are you going to do,
And where are you going to go
When you wake up tomorrow?

Have you thought about
What you will wear,
Or what you might eat,
Or who you will
Spend the day with?

When you lead a busy life,
There is so much
To think about.

If you wanted to,
You could probably
Spend half the night
Just thinking
About tomorrow!

But if you did that,
You wouldn't get
Much sleep.

If you get plenty
Of sleep,
You will have much more fun
Doing things
When you wake up.

Maybe it would be better,
If you put tomorrow
To bed!

Tell tomorrow good night.
You can really enjoy tomorrow
When you wake up.

Tell tomorrow
You will see it
Tomorrow!

"So don't be anxious about tomorrow. God will take care of your tomorrow, too. Live one day at a time." (Matt. 6:34, TLB)

The Day Is Over

It was a good day.
You had plenty to eat,
You had time to play,
And time to talk to someone
You like.

Some days are hard,
Or even sad,
But this day
Was a good day.

Now the day
Is over,
And this is
A good time
To be thankful.

Can you think
Of two things
That you would like
To thank your parents for?

It makes parents
Feel great
To know their children
Are thankful.

Can you think
Of two things
That you would like
To thank God for?

God likes to know
That people are thankful,
Too.

This is a
Terrific way
To end the day.

By being thankful!

"It is good to say 'Thank you' to the Lord." (Ps. 92:1, TLB)

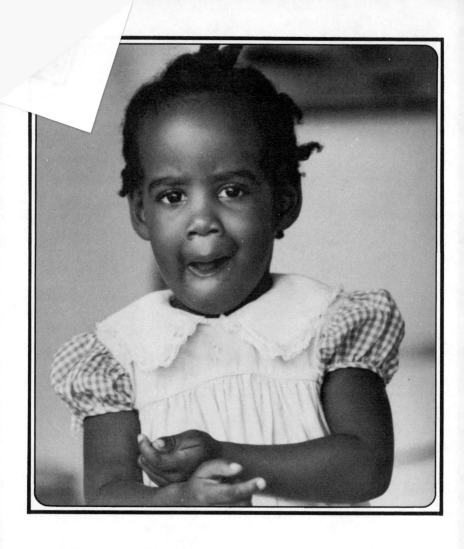

The Hair on Your Head

How would you describe
The hair on your head?

Is it short,
Or long?
What color
Is your hair?
Is it dark,
Or light?

Did you wash your hair
Before you went to bed?

Clean, soft hair
Is fun to comb
Into different shapes
And styles.

Do you ever part your hair
Down the middle,
Or try to make yourself
Look like a clown,
Or an old man,
Or a space captain?

Hair is good to have.
It is fun to play with,
And it feels warm
On a cold night
When the covers
Are pulled up tight.

Have you ever seen
A picture of yourself
When you were a baby?
What did your hair
Look like then?
Did you have a lot
Of hair,
Or did you have
Just a little?

Pull your blanket up
Over your ears
So just your hair
Is sticking out.

Now you can
Sleep tight.

**"And the very hairs of your head
are all numbered."** (Matt. 10:30, TLB)

A Parent's Arms

One of the most important things
In a child's life
Are the warm, strong arms
Of his parents.

Arms are great
For picking up
A child
When he can't see
A parade
Or when he can't reach
The ceiling.

Arms are good
When a child
Is very tired
And can't walk
Any farther.

Sometimes a strong parent
Will pick you up
And carry you for a while.

If you go to sleep
On the couch,
Or on the floor,
Or in a chair,
A parent
May pick you up
And carry you
To bed.

The best gifts in life
Are not toys.
They are not radios,

They are not
Electronic games.

The arms of a loving parent
At bedtime
Are one of the best
Gifts in life.

Tell everyone
Good night.

"The eternal God is your Refuge. And underneath are the everlasting arms." (Deut. 33:27, TLB)

Walking in Your Sleep

Have you ever heard of people
Who walk in their sleep?
Maybe you have walked in your sleep,
Or pretended you were.

Walking in your sleep
Doesn't happen too often.
Sometimes a person
Just gets out of bed,
Stands there for a few seconds,
And then climbs back
Into bed.

Sleepwalking is all right,
If you don't fall down
The stairs.

Most of us don't get up
In our sleep,
And if we do,
We don't do much walking.

If your brother or sister
Starts to walk
In his sleep,
It's all right
To wake him up.

You can quietly
Tell him
To go back to bed.

If you walk
In your sleep

Some night,
You probably won't
Remember it
The next day.

You will enjoy
Your night better
If you can
Stay in bed
All night long.

Have a good sleep.

"Rest in the Lord." (Ps. 37:7, TLB)

Telling Stories

Children aren't the only ones
Who enjoy hearing a good story.
Fathers, mothers, and others
Enjoy stories just as much.

We like stories from books,
Or stories on television.
We can also enjoy an exciting story
When someone just makes it up.

It is good to have
Someone read to us,
Especially at bedtime.

It's fun to hear about people,
Or birds, or dolphins,
Or coconut crabs, or monkeys.

If you have someone
That reads stories to you
At night,
You have someone special.
He must really like you
If he will read to you.

Jesus understood people,
And He liked them.
Maybe that is why
Jesus told so many stories.

He knew people would listen
To stories
And learn about God.

Jesus told stories about
Robbers,
Rich men,
Farmers,
Sheep,
Wolves,
Kings,
And
Many more.

Jesus must have been
A terrific storyteller.
Men, women, boys and girls
All liked to listen to Him.

Stories are fun.
Stories are easy.
Stories can tell us
More about God.

Be sure to thank the person
Who is reading to you.
Right now.

Good night,
Sleep tight.

"Jesus told several other stories to show what the Kingdom of Heaven is like." (Matt. 22:1, TLB)

Other Devotionals in this series

Counting Stars, meditations on God's creation.

My Magnificent Machine, lessons centered around the marvels of the human body.

Listen to the Animals, lessons from the animal world.

The Good Night Book, bedtime inspirationals (especially for those who may be afraid of the dark).

More About My Magnificent Machine, more devotionals describing parts of the human body and how they reflect the genius of the Creator.

On Your Mark, challenges from the lives of well-known athletes.

Today I Feel Like a Warm Fuzzy, devotionals for small children which help them to identify and learn how to respond to their own feelings and emotions.

Singing Penguins and Puffed-Up Toads, devotionals about the creatures of the sea.

Today I Feel Loved, devotionals that build self-esteem.